TOO MANY SECRETS

S TOO MANY SECRETS

BETTY REN WRIGHT

SCHOLASTIC INC.
New York Toronto London Auckland Sydney

ISBN 0-590-25236-4

12 11 10 9 8 7 6 5 4 3 2 1   8 9/9 0 1 2 3/0

Printed in the U.S.A.   40

First Scholastic paperback printing, May 1998

Book design by Elizabeth B. Parisi

For Beverly Butler Olsen,
who helped so much,
and for Benson,
outstanding waker-upper

Contents

TOO MANY SECRETS

ONE

Bad News

"That father of yours!" Chad Weldon's great-aunt Elsa set the phone down hard on the kitchen counter. "I could just smack him! Calling the last minute like this, when I have everything packed for the weekend!"

Chad took a step backward. Aunt Elsa was so angry her eyebrows bristled.

"We're not going to the cottage — again?" He waited for her grim nod. "Why not?"

"Same reason as last Friday night," Aunt Elsa snapped. "It's that play-acting of his. An extra re-hearsal, he says. I never saw such a man for going off without a thought for other people's feelings."

Chad felt like kicking something, but he didn't.

"Maybe we can go tomorrow morning," he suggested. "We could leave early. . . ."

"Not tomorrow either," his great-aunt replied crisply. She began emptying the cooler, slamming bottles and jars on the table. "Somebody's coming from Madison to teach the actors about makeup. A workshop, he calls it. A lot of nonsense, I call it. What's he need to learn about that for, anyway?"

Chad went outside, letting the screen door crash behind him. He plunked down on the back porch steps. Aunt Elsa got mad at his father at least once a month. That had been going on ever since she moved in to take care of them after Chad's mother died. But now Chad was as angry as she was. Usually he kept his anger bottled up a lot tighter than she did, but not this time.

"You're never home anymore," he growled, as if his dad were there to hear. "We never do stuff together. I don't care if you do have the biggest part in a dumb old play. I don't care!"

"When a person talks to himself that's the first sign he's going crazy," said Jeannie Nichols. She was peering at him around the corner of the house. "What don't you care about, crazy little boy?"

Chad scowled. Trust Jeannie to turn up when he wanted to be alone.

"We were supposed to go to Perch Lake this weekend," he grumped. "Now we're not. My dad's too busy."

"Busy with the play, I bet," Jeannie said. "And that's not all." She rolled her eyes mysteriously.

"What's that supposed to mean?"

Instead of answering, Jeannie asked another question. "So what are you going to do instead?"

"Who knows!" Chad had no idea what he was going to do this weekend, or for the next two weeks, until school started. It certainly looked as if there weren't going to be any more trips to Shaky Acres, the cottage on Perch Lake, until the play was over.

"Well, I'm going to be real busy," Jeannie said importantly, as if he'd been about to ask her to hang out with him. "I'm going to baby-sit Mrs. Corbett's twins for two hours in the morning and one hour in the afternoon. Too bad you're only nine. If you were eleven, maybe you could get a baby-sitting job, too, and earn some money."

Eleven isn't so grown-up, Chad thought disgustedly. She was right, of course, about nine being too young to get a job, but she didn't have to sound so pleased about it.

He stood up. "I'm going in," he said. Then, as he reached for the screen door, he remembered a question of his own. "What did you mean about my dad?" he demanded. "About his being busy with the play and that's not all."

Jeannie looked out over Aunt Elsa's vegetable garden with a dreamy expression on her thin, freckled face. "I'm not supposed to talk about it."

"About what?"

"About your father and Miss Calhoun. She's in the play, too. Mrs. Darby said Marcia Calhoun and your father make a lovely couple. My mother said maybe so, but I'm not supposed to gossip."

Chad blinked. He felt as if Jeannie had butted him in the stomach.

"That's stupid," he said, after a moment. The words came out sort of quivery, and for a horrible moment he thought he was going to cry. "That's the goofiest thing I ever heard of."

He opened the door and hurried inside. Aunt Elsa was on the telephone again as he streaked through the kitchen.

"Well, I don't know what to do about it, I'm sure," she was saying.

Me neither! Chad thought. *Whatever it is, I don't know what to do about it. I don't know what to do about* anything!

TWO

"I've Got a Job!"

"**Y**ou planning to starve yourself to death in there, or what?" Aunt Elsa spoke from the other side of the bedroom door.

Chad rolled over and studied the cracks in the ceiling. The more he thought about what Jeannie had told him, the worse he felt. And there was nothing else to think about.

"I'm not hungry," he said mournfully.

"Well, there's a problem we need to talk over," Aunt Elsa said. "Right now. Might as well eat at the same time."

Chad groaned. He wondered if Aunt Elsa had heard the gossip, too. She sounded more worried than angry now.

When he went out to the kitchen, he saw that the table was set — for two — with a platter of meat loaf and vegetables.

"I've just had the most dreadful news," Aunt Elsa announced as they sat down. "Dora Beane fell this morning and broke her ankle. That's your Miss Beane, young man," she went on impatiently, when Chad just stared. "Your Miss Beane from Sunday school. Now she's in the hospital, and after that she'll go to a nursing home, most likely, until she can get around on her own. I can hardly believe it!"

Chad helped himself to a slice of meat loaf. Lots of people fell down, especially old people, but he knew better than to say that. Aunt Elsa was sort of touchy about age.

"It wasn't just an ordinary fall," his aunt said sharply, as if she had been reading his mind. "She was hurrying downstairs because she thought she heard someone in her house. A burglar!"

"No kidding!" Chad looked up, interested. "Did she see who it was?"

"Not likely," Aunt Elsa retorted. "She bumped her head when she fell and never did wake up till she was in the hospital. The mail carrier saw her lying at the foot of the stairs, and he called the sheriff and an ambulance."

"She used to invite us to her house for chocolate cake and ice cream," Chad remembered. "I wonder what's going to happen to Benson and Baby."

"The dog and the parrot are with Mrs. Keck," Aunt Elsa said. "She has that little house next to Miss Beane's big one on Old Oak Road. That was her on the phone just now. She says she doesn't mind keeping the bird, but the dog Benson is too much. Taking him for walks and all — she says she doesn't have the time. She doesn't want to worry Dora, but she's all upset about it.

Chad made a path with his fork between his mashed potatoes and carrots. He could guess how Benson was feeling. Lonely. Bored. Unhappy.

Just like me.

"I could do it," he said suddenly. "I could take Benson for a walk every day. He could even stay with us if —" he put down his fork — "if it's okay with you and Dad."

"Your father isn't around enough lately to notice," Aunt Elsa said. "But I know it would make Dora feel a lot better if we took the dog. She told Mrs. Keck she wants to pay for the animal's care, wherever he ends up."

"You mean he really can come? Here?" Chad could hardly believe this was happening. He'd been wanting a dog for about a million years.

"Clean up your plate, and I'll call Mrs. Keck." Aunt Elsa's mouth twitched in a half-smile. "The quicker the better as far as she's concerned, I'm sure. It just so happens that's what we were talking about when you went rocketing into your bedroom."

Ten minutes later Chad dashed out the back door and around the side of the house. He raced down the block and was nearly at the corner when he heard Jeannie call from her porch across the street.

"Where do you think you're going?"

He glanced over his shoulder. She was starting down her front steps, but he waved her back.

"I'm in a hurry," he yelled, trying to sound off-hand about it. "See you later. I've got a job!"

THREE

"I Hear Something!"

"There could have been a burglar, I suppose." Mrs. Keck had a big, booming voice. "The dog is no watch-dog, that's for sure. He wouldn't bark if an army marched in the front door."

Chad followed her disdainful look to a corner of the dim little living room where Benson was curled into a large black ball. He was making a strange chopping sound.

"Biting his toenails," Mrs. Keck bellowed. "He's been doing that ever since the sheriff brought him here. Drives me wild! Biting his nails and moping. And the parrot's just as bad. She sits there in her cage with her head under her wing. But at least she doesn't take up much space."

"Hiya, Benson." Chad put out his hand. The big Labrador raised his head and looked unhappy.

"His leash is right there on the doorknob," Mrs. Keck hinted. "You'll have to pull him some to get him moving."

Chad hesitated. "Would it be okay if I talk to the parrot first?" he asked shyly. "She knows me, sort of."

Mrs. Keck sniffed and pointed toward the dining room. "You can talk to her," she boomed, "but she won't talk to you. Dora Beane claims she can talk, but I don't believe it. I've never heard her say a word."

Chad went into the dining room. He remembered that Miss Beane had told his Sunday school class to speak very softly if they wanted Baby to reply. The parrot had said, "Pretty bird," and "Time to go," and "Let's eat," and a lot of other things.

Today, though, the big green and yellow bird wouldn't even look up. Chad poked a finger through the bars of the cage to give Baby's head a gentle scratch. Then he went back to the living room where Mrs. Keck was waiting.

"You'd better go on home now," she said bluntly. "My favorite game show starts in one minute."

Chad snapped the leash to Benson's collar and

urged him to his feet. Outside, a warm wind had come up and the evening air had a fresh green smell. When they passed Miss Beane's house, Benson tried to turn up the walk and groaned loudly when Chad tugged him along the gravel road.

"Come on, boy." Chad stroked the slick black head. "You'll be okay." But Benson would not be comforted. Head and tail hanging limply, he let himself be led to Chad's house.

"Good grief!" Aunt Elsa shook her head when she saw him. "He looks like he's going to the gallows! You've got your work cut out for you, young man."

It was true. Benson seemed stunned at finding himself in still another unfamiliar house. Aunt Elsa fixed him a good dinner of table scraps, and Chad folded an old blanket to make a bed in the corner of his room, but the dog refused to eat or settle down. He was still prowling from room to room when Aunt Elsa said it was time for bed.

Chad was sleepy until he turned out the light. Then he was wide-awake. He wished Benson would come in and curl up on the blanket. Mostly, he wished Jeannie hadn't told him about his father and Miss Calhoun. Even having a dog to take care of wasn't enough to erase those scary words from his memory: *They make a lovely couple.*

Yuk!

Much later, Chad heard the family truck rattling into the driveway. He heard his dad's exclamation of surprise when he saw Benson, then the murmur of voices as Aunt Elsa explained. It helped a little to know his father was home, but still Chad couldn't sleep. Long after the rest of the house was dark, he lay awake listening to the *click-click* of Benson's toes as he wandered.

In the morning, the blanket-bed hadn't been slept on. Chad hurried out to the kitchen where Aunt Elsa was drinking her coffee.

"Where is he?"

"Behind the couch in the living room." Aunt Elsa sounded exhausted. "Follow your ears."

Chad listened. "He's biting his nails," he explained.

"I don't care what he's doing," Aunt Elsa snapped. "I just know I don't want to spend another night like this last one. That dog is a nervous wreck, and I'm going to be one, too, if he keeps it up. I'm beginning to think we made a big mistake saying we'd take him."

"No, we didn't," Chad said quickly. "He just has to get used to us."

Mr. Weldon came out to the kitchen, rubbing his

eyes. "Take him for a long, long walk, Chad," he suggested with a yawn. "Tire him out."

"I'm going to," Chad promised. "We'll play tug-of-war and stuff, too."

Aunt Elsa snorted. "That'll be like playing with a wet noodle," she said. "He's the least playful animal I've ever met."

Suddenly Chad remembered something that might be important. "Benson has a fuzzy bone he likes a lot," he said. "When we went to Miss Beane's house, he was always carrying it around. If I could get that . . ."

"A *fuzzy* bone?" Aunt Elsa made a face.

"Lamb's wool," Mr. Weldon murmured. "Bone-shaped. Washable."

"I guess Miss Beane's house is all locked up," Chad went on, his excitement fading.

"We can get in if I borrow a key from Dora," Aunt Elsa said. She poured coffee for Chad's father and refilled her own cup. "I was going to see her at the hospital this afternoon, anyway."

Chad wanted to say "Please go now," but he didn't. He knew his great-aunt couldn't be hurried once she had made plans. All he could do was wait.

It was a long day. After much coaxing, Benson

came out from behind the sofa. He ate a little of the dogfood Mr. Weldon brought home at noon, and he drank some water. But when Chad led him out to the backyard and threw a ball, the dog sighed and lay down, his chin on his paws. When Chad offered him one end of a rope to pull on, Benson closed his eyes.

Aunt Elsa was right. Cheering up Benson was going to be hard work.

At three-thirty Aunt Elsa came home from the hospital and handed Chad two keys. By that time Benson was behind the sofa again.

"Leave him, there," she suggested. "It's no use taking him back to his home and then dragging him away. Ask Jeannie to go with you. And be sure to lock up when you leave. Use both keys — one is for the regular locks and one is for the deadbolts on both doors. Dora says she never used the deadbolts much, but now she knows she should. She says she heard someone in the house before she fell. I told her maybe it was the dog, but she says he was asleep up in her bedroom, and the noises were downstairs. She vows she doesn't have money hidden in the house, but she said something else that sounded very odd. She said she has real treasure there, but no one would ever find it. That's why she hasn't bothered double-locking the doors." Aunt Elsa shook her head. "I don't know what to believe, I'm sure. The sheriff didn't find any sign that some-one had broken in."

Chad took the keys, but he was no longer sure that the fuzzy bone would make Benson happy. And the thought of going to Miss Beane's big, empty house scared him a little. He supposed he'd have to ask Jeannie to go along, even if she teased him about being afraid.

Fortunately, Jeannie wasn't in a mood to tease. "I'm going with you," she announced, before Chad had even explained why he was going to Old Oak Road. "I want to see the inside of Miss Beane's house. The twins' mom says she's rich."

Chad shrugged. Miss Beane's house seemed pretty ordinary to him, except for her collection, of course. He wondered what Jeannie would think about that.

"It's an awfully big house for one old lady," Jean-nie said in an almost-whisper as they turned up the front walk. She hung back just a little. "What did you say we're looking for?"

"A fuzzy bone. It's Benson's favorite thing." Chad was whispering, too — he didn't know why. He led the way up the porch steps and turned one of the keys in the old-fashioned lock. The door opened squeakily.

The very first thing Chad saw when they stepped inside was the fuzzy bone. It lay at the bottom of the staircase that led to the second floor.

"Look!" Chad pointed. "I bet Miss Beane stepped on it and fell when she came downstairs." He scooped up the bone and turned around.

Jeannie stood just inside the door, her eyes wide.

"SSSH!" she hissed. "I hear something!"

Chad stopped breathing.

"I don't hear anything. Quit trying to —"

He stopped, silenced by a rush of footsteps somewhere in the rear of the house. For a moment he was too frightened to move. Then he hurtled across the entrance hall and out the front door, shoving Jeannie ahead of him.

"Run!" he yelled and took off down the brick walk. He reached the road first, the only time he'd ever beaten Jeannie in a race. Of course, it was the only time he'd been quite that scared.

FOUR

Secrets

They crouched, panting, under a snowball bush, just out of sight of the house.

"You looked so funny, running with that bone in your hand like a scared puppy." Jeannie snickered. "What a stitch!"

"Didn't look any funnier than you did," Chad retorted. "You were scared, too."

"Was not." Jeannie peered out from under the bush. "Whoever it was is gone by now," she decided. "Let's go back and look for clues."

Chad followed her out into the road. He wanted to argue, but he knew Jeannie would call him chicken or baby if he refused to go back. Besides, he couldn't leave Miss Beane's house unlocked. That would be the first thing Aunt Elsa would ask about when he got home.

"Don't make any noise," Jeannie warned as they tiptoed up the front steps and crossed the porch for the second time. "Just in case. The burglar *might* still be there, but I don't think so. We scared him off."

What makes her so sure of everything? Chad wondered crossly.

The door stood open, as they had left it, and the little entrance hall was musty and hot.

"We'd better check the back door right away," Jeannie whispered. "He ran that way when he heard us coming. I'll go first —"

She broke off as she glanced into the living room. "Hey, look at that!"

In spite of his nervousness, Chad grinned. Jeannie was getting her first glimpse of Miss Beane's collection.

"Teddy bears!" she breathed. "I never saw so many teddy bears in my life."

Chad nodded. There were teddy bears in every chair and on the mantle and the hearth. Teddy bears peeked out from between books on the shelves, and more teddy bears sat in little groups in the corners. Some of them were huge, and others were no larger than a finger. Some wore bright costumes and looked brand-new, and some were battered old fellows with splitting sides, torn ears, and missing button-eyes.

For a moment longer they lingered in the hall, Jeannie staring into the living room and Chad keeping an anxious eye on the hallway that led to the kitchen and a back bedroom. The house was very still. It *felt* empty. But Chad's mouth was dry as he imagined a burglar hiding around a corner. He flattened himself against the wall, the way detectives did on television, and moved slowly along the hall and into the kitchen.

"Nobody here," he whispered. "And the back door's open. He must have tinkered with that old lock and sneaked in that way."

He took Miss Beane's keys from the pocket of his shorts and locked the old lock, then the sturdy deadbolt just above it. With the deadbolt fastened, the door couldn't be opened from the outside or the inside without a key.

"A teddy bear cookie jar," Jeannie said, strolling around the kitchen. "Teddy bear salt and pepper shakers. A teddy bear teapot, for pete's sake!"

Chad went to a window and looked out into the backyard. The row of tall lilac bushes at the side of the house continued all around the end of the yard. Close to the house, another row of bushes formed a hedge on either side of the porch.

"No footprints in the grass," he reported.

"Of course not," Jeannie scoffed. "But look way over there. That's really suspicious!" She pointed at the backs of three houses that faced the next street.

"Houses and trees," Chad said. "So what?"

"Look at that great big tree behind the middle house. Can't you see?"

Chad squinted. There was something in the tree, a sort of platform with low sides. "It's a treehouse," he said. "What's wrong about that?"

Jeannie looked disgusted. "What's wrong is that a person up in that treehouse could spy on this house whenever he wanted to — especially at night when the lights were on. He could tell when somebody was home real easily. And I know whose treehouse it is! It belongs to a kid called Cap Colby. That's what he calls himself — Cap. It's short for Captain, because he says he's going to work for NASA when he grows up and be the captain of a spaceship. We ought to go over there and question him right now."

Chad stared at her in amazement. "Just because he has a treehouse? How old is this kid?"

Jeannie shrugged. "Eleven or twelve, I guess. His mom teaches him at home, and he doesn't hang out with anybody special. I only know about the treehouse because I heard him bragging about it in the park one day."

"We'd better look around here first," Chad said. "Maybe we can find some real clues."

Together, they went from the kitchen into the dining room and then back to the living room. Jeannie admired the silver teddy-bear candlesticks and a funny little footstool in the shape of a crouching bear. On the other side of the hall was a smaller sitting room, and behind that a bedroom-workroom. A huge teddy bear dressed in a hand-knit sweater was perched in the middle of the bed.

Jeannie bent over something on the floor next to the bed. "It's a sewing box, and somebody has turned it upside down." She began gathering up spools of thread. "They've made a real mess," she commented. "We ought to have a fingerprint kit."

"It's too late now, anyway," Chad said. "You've got your prints all over it."

Jeannie gasped. "Look at this. There's a rip in the

lining of the box, and there's money tucked in the hole." She worked her fingers into the torn place and pulled out one five-dollar bill, then another one.

"Wow!" Chad could hardly believe it. "Miss Beane told my aunt that she didn't hide money in her house, so a burglar would be wasting his time."

"Well, she told your aunt a whopper," Jeannie said. "And I bet there was more money than this in the box. I bet the burglar was trying to get it out when we scared him off."

"Miss Beane wouldn't tell a whopper," Chad argued. "Maybe she forgot she put it there."

"And maybe there's more hidden all over this place," Jeannie retorted. She stuffed the bills back into the hole in the lining and pushed the sewing box out of sight under the bed. "That's what the burglar will think, too. He'll figure out some way to get in, and he'll keep coming back until he finds it all."

Chad hated the idea of a burglar searching through Miss Beane's things while she lay helpless in the hospital.

"We've got to tell my dad and Aunt Elsa right away," he said. "Or we can call the sheriff ourselves," he added. He liked that idea better. "We can tell him right now."

Jeannie stood up and glared at him, her hands on her hips. "Oh, sure we can," she said sarcastically. "Our one big chance to solve a crime and be heroes, and you don't even want to try."

"But we ought to tell someone," Chad protested. "We can't catch a burglar all by ourselves."

"How do you know? We can find out who he is, at least," Jeannie insisted. We can be a team — Nichols and Weldon, Detectives. Miss Beane might even give us a reward. Unless you can't keep a secret," she added slyly.

Chad stared at her. She was wrong and he knew it. They ought to tell. But she had said one word that sent his thoughts racing.

Secret.

His dad had a secret — a big one, that he was keeping from his family. It wasn't fair. It was mean. Chad clenched his fists, thinking about Marcia Calhoun.

"Okay," he said slowly. "We can do it. And we won't tell anybody. That's just fine with me."

FIVE

They're Going to Get Married!

"Hey, Benson, look at this." Chad knelt at one end of the couch and dangled the fuzzy bone where Benson could see it. There was a steady crunching sound from behind the couch.

Aunt Elsa watched from the kitchen door. "It won't work," she said.

Chad waved the bone up and down. "Come on, boy," he pleaded. "It's your bone. You love it!"

The crunching stopped. There was a scrambling sound as Benson struggled to his feet in the small space.

Chad dropped the bone on the floor and moved back. He held his breath as Benson poked the bone with his nose. He sniffed it, and then he picked it up in his big jaws and shook it fiercely.

"Good boy!" Chad exclaimed and was almost toppled over as Benson started cantering around the room. He dashed toward Aunt Elsa and darted away when she put out her hand and tried to touch the bone. Then he ran back to Chad and pretended to offer the bone to him, before darting away again.

"My stars and garters!" Aunt Elsa clapped her hands to her forehead. "It's like a miracle! That silly bone has turned him into a puppy again." She stepped to one side as Benson charged past her, with Chad right behind him.

"I'm going to teach him how to catch a Frisbee!" Chad shouted over his shoulder. He was glad to see Benson happy again, but he was even more pleased to have an excuse to get out of the house. Every time he looked at Aunt Elsa he felt guilty. If she knew they had heard someone prowling in Miss Beane's house . . . If she knew he and Jeannie were going to try to find out who the burglar was, without telling anyone else . . . His stomach felt funny, and for a moment he wished he hadn't promised Jeannie they could play detective. Then he thought of his dad, who wasn't coming home for dinner again tonight because there was an extra rehearsal at the theater. It's his fault, Chad thought. He threw the Frisbee so hard that it sailed behind the tomato plants.

Benson watched it fly by without interest. With his teeth fastened around the big bone he looked as if he were smiling. After a single gallop around the yard, he settled down under the maple tree with the bone between his front paws. Chad let him chew for a while, and then he fastened the leash to the dog's collar and took him for a walk. Benson carried the bone and looked around as if he wanted to make sure everyone saw him.

"Too bad we can't solve all our problems so easily," Aunt Elsa said that evening. "If I had one wish, I'd wish that silly play was over and done with and your father was home where he belongs."

Chad looked at her quickly, wondering if she was thinking about Marcia Calhoun. There was no way to tell. If Aunt Elsa had heard the gossip, she was keeping it to herself.

That night Benson curled up on his blanket-bed and slept with his nose resting on the fuzzy bone. And the next morning two big paws landed on the pillow close to Chad's head, and a cold nose tickled his chin.

"Too early," Chad muttered. He opened his eyes briefly and scratched Benson between the ears. A good smell wafted from the kitchen. Aunt Elsa was frying bacon, so it must be Sunday. He wished he were waking up at the cottage at Perch Lake. That was where he and his dad and Aunt Elsa belonged on weekends. If it weren't for the play — and Marcia Calhoun — that's where they would be. And this weekend would have been special fun because Benson would have been there with them.

"You'd love it Benson. We'd go swimming and we could hike in the woods. And maybe you could go fishing with us."

The thought of what he was missing stuck like a burr in Chad's mind through church and all the rest of the day. Having a dog was fun, but Benson liked lying in the shade better than chasing a ball. After they went for a walk there wasn't much else to do with him. As the afternoon and evening dragged by, Chad felt more and more sorry for himself. That night he dreamed his father sold the cottage because Marcia Calhoun didn't like it.

Monday morning he awoke to the sound of Aunt Elsa's and Jeannie's voices out in the kitchen. He dressed quickly, stopping once to rub Benson's chest when the big dog ambled into the bedroom carrying his bone.

"I don't have to baby-sit until eleven today, so I'm going to help you walk Benson," Jeannie announced. She made it sound as if she were doing Chad a favor, but he didn't care. If he had company, he wouldn't have to worry about his dad's secret. And he wouldn't have to think about his own secret, either. Jeannie would keep reminding him how great it would be to solve the mystery at Miss Beane's house all by themselves.

"You can't let Benson take the bone with him," she protested when they started out after breakfast. "He'll drop it somewhere."

"No, he won't," Chad said. "He can take it if he wants to." He said it firmly, to show that taking care of Benson was his job, not hers.

"Is it okay if we walk downtown?" Jeannie asked, sounding a little less bossy. "I have to go to the drugstore for my mom."

Chad agreed, but later he was sorry. People kept laughing at the way Benson looked, with the big bone hanging from his mouth.

He was about to say he and Benson would wait for Jeannie on a bench in the middle of the town

square, away from most passersby, when he saw
something startling. His dad's truck was parked in
front of Gorman's Furniture Store.

Jeannie saw the truck as soon as he did.

"What's going on?" she demanded. "I thought
your father was working."

Chad had thought so, too. "Maybe he had an errand," he said doubtfully.

"Let's go and look," Jeannie said. "He might be
buying some new stuff for your cottage."

Chad didn't think so. They didn't have extra
money for new furniture. Besides, the cottage at
Shaky Acres was fine exactly the way it was.

Reluctantly, he followed Jeannie across the
square to the furniture store. They pressed their
noses up against the glass and squinted, while Benson stretched out on the sidewalk.

"He's back there." Chad pointed to the rear of the
store. "Talking to somebody."

Jeannie gasped. "And I know who it is!" she exclaimed. "That's Marcia Calhoun with him. Look at
her — she's really pretty!"

Chad didn't want to look. He turned his back to
the window.

"Who cares?" he said. "Let's go."

But Jeannie was already darting toward the door. "I'm going to investigate," she said excitedly. "You wait here and I'll tell you what's going on."

"I don't want to know what's going on!" Chad shouted. "I'm leaving!"

He pulled Benson to his feet and stomped down the street, past the Bristol Grill and the shoe repair shop. At the corner he looked back, hoping Jeannie had returned. He hated her for charging into the store like that. What his family did was none of her business. Yet at the same time, he wanted desperately to know why his dad was in the furniture store with that *person*.

It seemed forever before Jeannie finally reappeared. The cap, that she usually wore on the back of her head, was pulled down over her forehead.

"They never even noticed me!" she said triumphantly. "I got up real close. They were so busy they never even noticed."

Chad stared at her, waiting.

"And I'll tell you what they're doing," she continued, pushing the cap back to its usual position. "They're buying a kitchen table and chairs, that's what!"

"Big deal," Chad said.

Jeannie shook her head, as if he'd just said the

dumbest thing she'd ever heard. "Don't you know *anything*?" she demanded. "When people start buying stuff like that, it's serious. Before you even know it, they're married. You're going to wake up some morning with a brand-new mother!"

Without even thinking about what he was doing, Chad gave Jeannie a hard shove. Then he turned around and ran as fast as he could, dragging Benson behind him.

SIX

Detective at Work

"Jeannie's on the phone," Aunt Elsa called from the back door. "She wants to talk to you."

Chad threw the Frisbee one more time and gave up. Benson didn't understand about Frisbees. Each time Chad threw it, Benson waited till it landed, then carried it to a shady corner of the yard and dropped it there.

"Why in the world does she call you?" Aunt Elsa wondered, when Chad came into the kitchen. "She's just across the street, for goodness' sake."

Chad was pretty sure he knew why. Jeannie wanted to yell at him for pushing her, but she didn't want Aunt Elsa to hear. He picked up the telephone with a sigh.

"Yeah?"

"I'm sorry I said that about your getting a new mom." She did sound unhappy. "I mean, it's probably true, but I shouldn't —"

"Forget it," Chad said gruffly.

"So," Jeannie went on softly, as if she guessed Aunt Elsa was right there listening while she mixed cookie dough, "are you sorry for the mean thing *you* did?"

"Yeah," Chad said. "I am."

"And are we still going to be detectives and find out who Miss Beane's burglar is? All by ourselves?"

Chad hesitated only a moment. If the burglar came back and he and Jeannie could identify him, they would be heroes. He imagined his dad's amazement when he read the newspaper headline:

BRISTOL KIDS GET MEDALS

"It's okay with me," he muttered. "See you tomorrow."

"No, not tomorrow," Jeannie became her bossy self again. "Tomorrow is my grandpa's birthday, and we're having a big party. I have to help my mom clean and stuff when I'm through baby-sitting."

Chad bit his lip. "I'll go to Miss Beane's myself then," he said. He didn't want to go alone, but what if the burglar came back, and no one was there to see him?

"What's on your mind, young man?" Aunt Elsa demanded when he had hung up. "You look scowly."

"I'm okay," Chad said. "Is Dad coming home for supper?"

Aunt Elsa cleared her throat, as if she wanted to be careful of what she said. "There's an early rehearsal," she said. "They're going to have pizza delivered to the theater."

Chad turned to look at her. Last week she'd been furious with his dad because he was spending so much time on the play. Now she was acting as if it didn't matter. She knew about Marcia Calhoun, he decided. Maybe she didn't know his dad and Miss Calhoun were buying a kitchen table together, but she was worried and was trying to keep the worry to herself.

That evening Jeannie came over and they sat on the front steps with Benson between them. "I just wish I didn't have that baby-sitting job," Jeannie grumbled. "Too bad I'm so good at it — I think the twins' mother would just about die if I quit."

Chad rolled his eyes. "You don't have to quit," he said. "I'm going to watch Miss Beane's house tomorrow."

"I wish we could go tonight," Jeannie said. "That would be really exciting — and scary! We could take flashlights and —"

"Well, we can't," Chad interrupted impatiently. "If the burglar comes back, he'll probably come in the daytime anyway. It was morning that first time when Miss Beane heard him prowling around. And it was afternoon when we almost caught him before he ran away."

"And I bet I know why," Jeannie announced. "Cap Colby's parents won't let him go out at night, any more than ours will. He's really a good suspect! He can see a long way from that treehouse. You'll have to keep out of sight when you're on guard."

"I know that," Chad snapped. "You don't have to tell me everything."

"You're not going to take Benson, are you? He'll bark and spoil everything."

Chad hadn't thought about it, but he was tired of taking orders.

"I'm taking him," he said flatly. "He won't bark with his bone in his mouth. And if I left him home, Aunt Elsa would want to know where I was going.

Besides, walking him is my job, same as baby-sitting is yours."

He didn't add that having Benson along would make him feel a lot braver. They would be partners, a detective and his fierce dog.

Actually, it took a lot of pretending to think of Benson as fierce. For one thing, the way he pulled his lips back in order to hold the big bone made him look as if he were smiling all the time. And in the second place, he rested a lot. Three times on their way across town the next afternoon he stretched out on the sidewalk and nuzzled his bone. He would have stayed there all afternoon if Chad hadn't dragged him to his feet.

By the time they reached Old Oak Road, Chad was tingling with impatience.

"Now listen," he said firmly as they turned onto the narrow road. "You have to do just what I do. The trees and bushes hide us pretty well here, but when we get closer to Miss Beane's house, we'll have to crawl in the ditch. Keep your head down."

Benson knew the word *down*. He stretched out on the dusty grass and yawned.

"No, NO!" Chad yanked the leash. "Get up, dopey! Heel! Move!"

Benson looked up reproachfully but did as he

was told, gripping the fuzzy bone tightly. Slowly they moved forward, with Chad stopping to peer between the trees every few steps. Twice he glimpsed Cap Colby's treehouse in the distance. Each time, he dropped to his knees and crawled, pulling Benson down with him.

When they reached the edge of Miss Beane's yard, Chad slid into the drainage ditch. This was going to be the tricky part. The ditch was shallow, damp, and musty-smelling, but it would hide them completely if they kept their heads down.

"We're going to crawl all the way to that row of lilac bushes between this yard and Mrs. Keck's," he explained to Benson, "and then we're going to make a run for the bushes and hide underneath them. We can watch the front yard and the back-yard from there."

Benson cocked his head. He looked puzzled, but willing. Together they worked their way along the ditch, until the long row of lilac bushes was only a few feet away.

Chad peeked over the edge of the ditch one more time. He could see just a corner of Cap Colby's tree-house.

"Okay," he breathed. "Get ready. Run!"

He scrambled up out of the ditch and dived

under the bushes. *Cool!* he thought, when his heart stopped thudding. Too bad Jeannie hadn't been there to see him.

Then he realized that Benson was no longer with him. The leash stretched out across the grass and down into the ditch.

"Hey!" he whispered hoarsely, and tugged at the leash. "Come on!"

There was a mournful yelp.

"Be quiet! Get up here — come!"

Benson's big black head rose from the ditch. He yelped again. His mouth was empty. He had lost his bone, and he wasn't going any farther without it.

Chad groaned. He could hear Jeannie saying I-told-you-so, as clearly as if she were crouched there under the bushes beside him.

SEVEN

"Benson Did It!"

Benson was no help at all in finding the bone. He whimpered and snorted while Chad crawled through the ditch, digging into the matted weeds at the bottom.

"Some detective you are!" Chad muttered. "Be quiet, will you!" Then he gave a little yelp himself, as one hand plunged into a puddle of slimy water. His finger closed around something at the bottom — the bone!

"Okay, dopey, here it is." He held out the dripping bone, and Benson leaped joyfully to grab it. Two big paws knocked Chad's other arm from under him, and down he went, face first, into the murky puddle.

"Yuk! Now look what you've done!" Chad wrapped the leash around his waist and crawled back to the end of the ditch, then up over the edge, into the shelter of the lilac bushes. This time Benson followed happily.

"Stay under the bushes," Chad warned him. "And keep quiet. We're going back far enough so we can see the backyard."

It was hot in the tunnel-like space beneath the lilacs. Mosquitoes buzzed, and tiny gnats tickled Chad's nose. Benson chomped on the wet bone contentedly. He didn't seem to notice that he was spying on his own house.

By parting the branches just a little, Chad could see most of Miss Beane's backyard. Leaning the other way, he could see a little of the walk that led to her front door. Not that a burglar was likely to stroll up the front path, of course, but a good detective had to think of everything.

"If he comes, he'll probably sneak through the bushes in the back," Chad whispered. "He won't know the deadbolt is locked, so he'll try the door first. Then he might break a window. . . ." He leaned out a little farther, wishing he could catch another glimpse of Cap Colby's treehouse. At this very minute Cap might be up there, getting ready to try his luck as a burglar again.

Minutes slipped by. "I s'pose he could have given up," Chad admitted. "But if he does come, we'll be ready, right?"

Benson yawned and closed his eyes.

Slowly, the tree shadows lengthened across the lawn. *We must have been here a couple of hours,* Chad thought. Jeannie would say a couple of hours were nothing, but she wasn't the one with gnats up her nose and sweat running down the back of her neck. He brushed away a huge spider that was crawling over his sneaker, and at that moment he felt himself being lifted by the shoulders.

He flew through the air and landed with a thump in front of a pair of very long trouser-legs.

"What do you think you're doing, buster?" demanded a deep voice. "What are you up to?"

Back under the lilac bushes, Benson woke to find himself alone. He began to bark. Chad scrambled to his feet and looked up at the tall young man glowering at him.

"I wasn't up to anything!" he exclaimed. "I'm guarding Miss Beane's house."

"Guarding her house?" The man laughed unpleasantly. He had thick black curls and he wore a bandanna, like a pirate. "More likely you're looking for a way to break in."

"I was not! Miss Beane's my friend. I'm helping her!"

Benson chose that moment to crash through the bushes, clutching his bone and dragging his leash behind him.

"This is her d-dog," Chad stammered excitedly. "I'm taking care of him, too. You can ask Mrs. —"

"It's all right, Jay." Mrs. Keck's bellow from her back porch was the most welcome sound Chad had ever heard. "Jay's my nephew, Chad. He's helping me with my yard work for a couple of days."

"He *says* he's guarding Miss Beane's house," Jay Keck told her. "Why should it need guarding?"

"Because —" Chad started to say the house had already been broken into at least twice, but he stopped just in time. If he told the Kecks about the burglar, they'd probably call the sheriff right away. Jeannie would be furious, and their chance to solve the mystery would be gone. "Because lots of people know Miss Beane's in the hospital," he finished carefully. "Somebody might decide to steal her stuff."

Mrs. Keck gave a great, booming laugh. "Well, they'd be wasting their time," she said. "I doubt there's much market for stolen teddy bears — not in Bristol, anyway."

Chad slapped at a mosquito. "Some people say she has money hidden in her house."

"I doubt that," Mrs. Keck said firmly. "Now you'd better take the dog and run along, Chad, because there's a lot to do around here, and Jay has to go to his regular job in a little while. We don't have time to stand around gabbing."

Jay Keck bent and picked up the end of Benson's leash. "Don't forget your guard dog," he said and winked.

Chad was glad to go. He grabbed the leash and was heading toward the road when he saw Baby the parrot at one of Mrs. Keck's windows. Her head was scrunched between her shoulders and her feathers were ruffled. She looked miserable.

He turned back to Mrs. Keck. "How's Baby?"

Mrs. Keck waved a hand impatiently. "All right, I guess. She ought to be, with all the work I put in taking care of her. I thought it would be fun to have a parrot, but that one just mopes. And messes up her cage."

Poor Baby! "Maybe she's lonesome," Chad suggested timidly. "Would it be okay if I went in and talked to her? Just for a minute?"

Mrs. Keck shrugged. "I suppose so. But don't expect any answers. And leave the dog out here. I don't want him carrying that filthy wet *thing* into my house."

Chad looped Benson's leash around a tree branch. "I'll be right back," he promised and hurried into the house before Mrs. Keck could change her mind.

Baby was in the dining room. When Chad came in, she turned to him with a mournful expression.

"Hi, Baby." Chad spoke very softly, the way Miss Beane had taught him. "Don't feel bad, girl. Miss Beane will be back." He opened the door of the cage and reached in to stroke the cap of soft feathers.

Baby made a chuckling sound.

"Everything will be okay," Chad whispered. "My friend Jeannie and I are going to find out who's breaking into your house."

Baby moved closer. She cocked her head as if she understood every word.

Chad hated to leave her, but he didn't want Mrs. Keck and Jay to come looking for him. He closed the cage and started for the kitchen. Maybe Mrs. Keck would let him come back another day and cheer up the parrot again.

He had almost reached the back door when Baby spoke at last.

"Bad Benson," she said. "Bad, bad Benson. Benson did it!"

EIGHT

Too Many Worries

"Benson did *what*?"

"I don't know what. That's just what Baby said."

Chad and Jeannie sat on the Weldons' front steps eating Aunt Elsa's pecan cookies. Chad was sorry he'd told her what happened that afternoon. When he described how Benson had lost his bone, Jeannie had said, "I warned you." When he told her that Jay Keck had grabbed him and dragged him out of the bushes, she'd laughed. And now, when he got to the really mysterious thing Baby had said, she acted as if she didn't believe him.

"Listen," he said crossly, "I told Baby we were going to find out who the burglar was, and that was when she said it. 'Bad Benson. Benson did it.' That has to mean something. Don't forget, Baby was there when someone broke into the house and Miss Beane fell."

Jeannie wound a strand of hair around her finger. "I don't believe Baby understood what you were saying. A parrot can't think like a person."

"This one can," Chad insisted. "She knew, all right."

"Well," Jeannie shrugged, "when you go back to-morrow, talk to her again. Maybe she'll tell you more."

"I can't tomorrow. Aunt Elsa wants me to go with her when she gets groceries, and in the afternoon I have to weed the garden."

"But you *must* go back tomorrow," Jeannie wailed. "What if the burglar shows up, and we aren't there?"

"You wouldn't be there anyway," Chad pointed out. "And Mrs. Keck's nephew is helping her in the yard for a couple of days, so he'll probably be watching. He sure was watching yesterday!" He rubbed his bruised shoulder where Jay Keck had grabbed him.

"The day after tomorrow then," Jeannie said. She stood up and dusted the seat of her shorts. "I don't have to baby-sit Thursday because the twins' grandma is coming for a visit. We can both guard the house all day. I bet we'll catch the burglar — and it won't be Benson either. What a stitch!"

Chad's face burned as he watched her cross the street. "You don't know everything," he muttered. "Baby's a smart bird, and she was trying to give me a clue. I just have to figure out what it is."

"Your father's going to be home for dinner for a change," Aunt Elsa told him, when he wandered back into the house. "No rehearsal tonight. So don't eat all the cookies."

"I won't." Chad went into his bedroom and took out his box of baseball cards. He hoped his dad wouldn't ask what he'd been doing all day. He could say, "I took Benson for a walk." Or, "I talked to Mrs. Keck and her nephew." But telling one little part of the truth felt a lot like lying.

As it turned out, he needn't have worried. His father didn't ask what he'd been doing. He didn't even mention that the stuffed pork chops tasted good, though they were his favorite food. He was too busy talking about the play and Marcia Calhoun.

"She is so great in her part," he told them excitedly. "Wait'll you see her! She can sing and dance, and she reads her lines better than anyone else in the cast. We're really lucky she's moving to Bristol.

She makes the rest of us sound better because she's so good."

"Where does she live now?" Aunt Elsa asked, without looking up from her dinner.

"In Madison. She's rented a room here for the summer, but she's going to move here soon. She'll be teaching first grade in your school, Chad. You'll like her."

Chad spooned some applesauce onto his plate. "I probably won't ever see her," he said. "First graders are babies."

He sounded rude, and he didn't care. It was awful, the way his dad kept talking about Marcia Calhoun, never noticing that Chad and Aunt Elsa didn't want to listen.

After supper Aunt Elsa went to the hospital to visit Miss Beane, and the Weldons played catch in the backyard. It should have been fun, but it wasn't. Chad's father kept looking at his watch.

"After we finish with this," he said, "I have to study my lines for a while. You can help me, Chad. You can read the other parts and give me my cues."

Chad reached for an easy ball and missed it.

"I'd just as soon quit now," he said sourly. "There's a show I want to see on TV."

For the first time, Mr. Weldon seemed to hear the

anger in Chad's voice. "Okay," he said slowly. "What are you going to watch?"

Chad shrugged. "Just a show." He hurried into the house before his dad could ask any more questions.

When Aunt Elsa came home an hour later, Chad was staring at the television set with Benson curled up on the sofa beside him. A herd of cows was galumphing across the screen in a cloud of dust.

Aunt Elsa watched for a moment. "Didn't know you were a western fan," she said. "Where's your father?"

"In his bedroom. Studying his part for the play." Chad kept his eyes on the cows.

"Oh." Aunt Elsa sat down in the recliner and kicked off her shoes. "Miss Beane said to say hello to you. She wanted me to thank you for looking after Benson. She said you were a good friend."

A friend who knows someone's trying to steal her money but doesn't tell anybody, Chad thought. He scrunched deeper into the sofa and wished people would stop telling him things he didn't want to hear.

NINE

"The Burglar Could Be in There."

It rained on Thursday, but even in the rain it was easier sneaking up on Miss Beane's house without Benson. Chad showed Jeannie how to dart from tree to tree along the gravel road, so that someone coming out of Mrs. Keck's driveway, or watching from Cap Colby's treehouse, wouldn't see them. But when they reached the ditch at the edge of Miss Beane's lawn, Jeannie stopped short.

"No way!" she exclaimed. "I'm not going in there . . . it's filling up with water!"

"So what?" Chad said boldly. "Who cares about a little rain?"

Jeannie edged back under the snowball bush where they'd hidden once before. "In the first place, it isn't a *little* rain. It's a whole lot. And in the second place, I don't see why we're worrying about anyone seeing us. Mrs. Keck and her nephew won't be out in the yard today. And Cap Colby probably isn't up in his treehouse either."

Chad sighed. She was right. Still, he would have liked to make her crawl through the ditch, the way he'd done it.

"It's a good thing you brought the house keys," Jeannie went on. "We couldn't stand guard outside, that's for sure."

Chad didn't want to think about the keys. Keeping quiet about the burglar was bad enough, but taking Miss Beane's keys without Aunt Elsa's permission was just as wrong. Maybe worse.

Jeannie crawled out to the road and stood up. "All clear," she reported. "Let's make a run for the house. But be quiet going up the steps. The burglar could already be in there, you know."

She dashed off across the lawn, her long legs stretched in the giant steps that made her the fastest runner in Bristol Elementary. Chad followed, almost but not quite keeping up. They went up the porch steps on tiptoe, crouching in case someone glanced out a window.

Chad opened the two locks with shaky fingers.

He felt as if Aunt Elsa were looking over his shoulder. They slipped inside, and Jeannie eased the door shut behind them.

"Look!" she whispered, pointing into the living room. "The sofa! The cushions are messed up." She clutched Chad's arm, and they stood like statues, hardly daring to breathe.

Chad wished he'd stayed home. Suddenly, he didn't want to be a detective. He didn't want to catch the burglar in the act.

Seconds slipped by, and there was no sound in the old house. Chad began to feel better. The burglar could have searched the sofa yesterday. Or he could have broken in the day before yesterday, after Baby had finally talked and the Kecks had sent Chad home.

"I'll check the back windows," he whispered. "Maybe he forced one open and went out the same way."

He tiptoed down the hall to the kitchen. On sunny days it was a bright, cheerful room, but today, with the rain beating against the panes, it looked gloomy. Even the teddy-bear cookie jar wore a grim expression.

The windows weren't broken. Chad tried the door and found both locks fastened.

"We'd better check all the downstairs windows," Jeannie said from the doorway.

Cautiously they moved from room to room. In the back bedroom, they discovered the sewing box pulled out from under the bed. The money that had been hidden in the lining was gone. In the living room they found that it was not just the sofa cushions that had been moved. Books had been taken off the shelves and left on the floor. Some of the teddy bears were tumbled on their sides. The little knapsack one of them wore had been opened.

Chad tried not to think of how unhappy Miss Beane would be if she knew what was happening in her house.

"We'd better straighten things up," he said miserably, but Jeannie shook her head.

"Better not. After we catch the burglar, the sheriff can check his fingerprints and prove he did all this. I'll keep looking for clues here," she added. "You check the basement."

"The basement!"

"Well, sure. He might have gotten in that way, right?"

And he might still be down there. With dragging steps, Chad returned to the kitchen. There was a little back hall, where a flight of stairs came down from the second floor and another flight led to the basement. He stared down into the darkness for a moment and felt around for a light switch. Then he returned to the living room.

"There aren't any basement windows," he said. "And I can't find the switch. Go see for yourself."

Jeannie looked at him. "It doesn't really matter anyway," she decided. "The important thing is to catch the burglar. After we get him, he can tell us how he broke in."

"I think we should call the sheriff," Chad said stubbornly. "He'll know what to do."

"I know what to do, too."

Chad wanted to argue, but he realized it was a waste of time. Jeannie's face was pink with excitement. She was tapping one foot, which was what she did when she was about to make things worse than they already were.

TEN

"I Told You So!"

"What we have to do is talk to Cap Colby," Jeannie announced. "Maybe we can trick him into confessing."

Chad groaned. "That's dumb. Why would he confess to us?"

"Because." Jeannie clearly didn't have an answer. "If you call the sheriff now, we'll be in big trouble," she argued. "First you'll have to tell him we knew someone was breaking in here. And then you'll have to tell him we broke in ourselves."

Chad gasped. "We didn't break in," he protested.

"Yes, we did. You took the keys and used them without asking. That's the same as breaking in. Of course, if we catch the burglar, nobody'll ever think of all that. We'll be heroes. Wouldn't you rather be a hero?"

"Well, sure, but —" Once again, Chad wished he were home. Throwing a Frisbee for Benson in the rain would be better than this. "Cap Colby won't be up in his treehouse when it's raining," he argued. "You said that yourself."

"Better yet," Jeannie retorted. "It'll give us a chance to search for clues." She had answers for everything.

"You lock the front door from the inside, and I'll duck out the back," she ordered. "It'll be better if we sneak across the the yard one at a time. Just in case somebody's watching."

Grumbling, Chad did as he was told. At least her plan took them out of the house. When he stepped out on the back porch, he could see Jeannie waiting under the bushes at the end of the yard. He crouched and ran.

Together, they squeezed through the tall, leafy wall. On the other side, the Colby's backyard was bordered by clusters of daisies and mums. At the far end, close to the house, was a huge maple. The treehouse stretched across the three broad branches.

"He isn't there," Jeannie murmured. "I can tell."

They crept closer, their eyes on the treehouse. Thick strands of plastic cord held the base of the house firmly in place. Around the sides, wooden slats about a foot high formed low walls. There was a green canvas roof propped up by poles in each corner.

"Come on," Jeannie urged Chad toward the ladder.

We're breaking in again, he thought, but when Jeannie started up the ladder he was close behind her. She was probably right; if they stopped now, without discovering who the burglar was, they'd be in big trouble. He would be, at least. Jeannie would probably be able to talk her way out of that, too.

"Hey, this is great!" Jeannie scrambled up through the hole in the treehouse floor. "I'm going to get my dad to build me a house like this."

"Me, too!" For a moment Chad forgot how worried he was. The treehouse was like a boat that sailed on air instead of water. "I'm going to have mine at Perch Lake," he decided. "Where I can look out over the water and watch the eagles." Then he remembered that his father was too busy these days to go to the lake. When would he ever have time to build a treehouse there?

Rain pattered pleasantly on the canvas roof. There was a fat beanbag chair on the platform and a box with a plastic sheet folded over it. A net bag full of soft-drink cans lay in the corner.

Jeannie pulled the plastic sheet off the box.

"Hey, that's his private stuff," Chad protested.

Jeannie frowned. "Why'd we come up here if we aren't going to look for clues?" She reached into the box and pulled out a pair of expensive binoculars. "I told you so! Cap can look right into Miss Beane's back windows with these. And there's all kinds of books in here. Some of them look brand-new — I bet he used the sewing-box money to buy them."

"What kind of books?"

Jeannie shrugged. "Birds, bugs — there's a big book about stars and stuff. And here's one that says —"

"WHO'S UP THERE?"

Chad leaped back from the opening in the floor of the treehouse. Jeannie dropped the book she was holding.

"It's Cap!" she muttered. "We're trapped!"

"GET OUT OF THERE! YOU'RE ON PRIVATE PROPERTY. YOU'RE GOING TO JAIL!"

Chad peered over the edge of the opening and

looked down into the boy's face that was red with fury.

"We're coming," he said quickly. He turned and stepped backward onto the ladder. Jeannie followed. A moment later they were face-to-face with Cap Colby.

"A couple of dumb kids! You've got a lot of nerve! What were you doing up there?" There were tears of rage in his squinty blue eyes.

Cap was big — almost as tall as Chad's father. If he was twelve, he was the biggest twelve-year-old in Bristol.

"We just wanted to see what it was like," Jeannie said. "We were over at Miss Beane's house and we saw your treehouse so —"

"Miss Beane's not home," Cap growled. He pushed his bright red baseball cap to the back of his head. "She's in the hospital."

"How do you know?" Jeannie demanded. "Were you spying on her?"

Chad shivered. She was going to get both of them killed.

"I know it because I saw the ambulance take her away. She's a friend of mine — not that it's any of your business. What were *you* doing over there?"

Chad closed his eyes and prayed that Jeannie wouldn't tell him.

"We were detecting," she said proudly. "Somebody's been getting into her house and stealing stuff. We're looking for clues."

"So what's that got to do with me?" Cap Colby's broad face got even redder than it had been before. His huge hands curled into fists. "You were looking for clues in my treehouse?"

Chad decided he was about to have his first fight. And he was going to lose.

"We just wanted to see what it was like," he said hoarsely. "It's really neat."

Suddenly Cap Colby shoved his way between them and started up the ladder. "Just get out of here," he snarled. "And don't come back. If you do, you'll be sorry."

"We won't! Honest!" Chad grabbed Jeannie's hand, and they raced across the lawn to the row of bushes that separated the two yards. When they had scrambled through, Jeannie collapsed on the ground, giggling.

"Did you see his face?" she gasped. "We've really got him worried!"

Chad was amazed. "He didn't look worried to me.

He looked mad! Why didn't you tell me how big he was? You could have gotten us beaten up, all for nothing."

Jeannie sat up and grinned her I-told-you-so grin. "It wasn't all for nothing," she said. "Wait'll you hear!"

"If you mean the binoculars," Chad said, "that's not a clue. Anybody could have binoculars."

"Not the binoculars," Jeannie retorted. "It's much more important than that. I saw Cap's name taped on the cover of one of his books — his *real* name. And now it all fits together like a detective story."

Chad frowned. "What do you mean?"

"His real name," Jeannie said slowly, "is Benton Colby. Get it?"

"No!"

Jeannie jumped to her feet. "That's what Baby the parrot was trying to tell you, dopey. 'Benton did it,' — *Benton,* not Benson! Cap said Miss Beane is a friend of his, and that means he's probably been in her house lots of times. And if he was, I bet she calls him Benton, not Cap. So that's what Baby would call him, too!"

ELEVEN

Nightmare!

Chad was relieved, and proud, too. He'd uncovered an important clue, and Jeannie had figured out what it meant. Weldon and Nichols had solved their case, and now they could stop being detectives.

"Who's going to call the sheriff?" he asked on the way home. "You or me?"

Jeannie looked at him sharply. "Neither one. The sheriff won't believe a parrot, dopey. You and I know who Baby's talking about, but we still have to catch Cap in the house. You watch by yourself tomorrow," she added casually. "I have to baby-sit."

Chad kicked a pebble. He didn't want to go back

to Miss Beane's house again. He certainly didn't want to go alone.

"Let the sheriff watch," he grumbled. "That's his job."

Jeannie made a face. "Do it for a little while, at least," she coaxed. "We might get lucky."

"What do you mean 'we'?" Chad demanded. "If I go, it'll just be for a couple of hours. Maybe not even that long. I have stuff to do, too, you know."

"Like what?"

Chad didn't answer. He was pleased when he got home and Aunt Elsa gave him the excuse he was looking for.

"You and I are going to give the garage a good cleaning tomorrow morning," she announced. "The clutter is driving me crazy, and if I wait for your father, it'll never get cleaned up." She shook her head. "He called to say he's eating at the theater again tonight. He said you and I were welcome to come and watch the rehearsal, if we want to. He'd like us to meet the cast."

"I'd rather watch television," Chad said quickly.

"I thought that'd be your answer." Aunt Elsa gave him a funny little smile. "I told him not to expect us."

It was a long evening. When Chad wasn't thinking

about his dad and Marcia Calhoun, he was worrying about going back to Miss Beane's tomorrow afternoon.

"You look as if you have all the troubles of the world on your head," Aunt Elsa commented at nine o'clock. "Maybe a good night's sleep will help."

Chad didn't think so. He was angry and scared at the same time. Sleeping wouldn't change that.

When he finally fell asleep, he dreamed he was in Miss Beane's house, standing in the hallway. On the other side of the wall, something big was tromping around the living room, bumping into furniture and snarling. A real detective would try to find out what the something was but Chad couldn't make himself look. Instead, he closed his eyes tightly until the noises stopped.

When he opened them, he stared up into a huge, hairy brown face. The glaring eyes were like shiny black buttons, and a dripping red tongue lolled between pointed teeth.

It was a bear — a teddy bear — six feet tall and very much alive.

Chad screamed, and screamed again. He woke as Aunt Elsa burst into his bedroom.

"What in the world, Chad!" she exclaimed. "Were you having a nightmare?"

Chad nodded. His heart thudded so hard it hurt, and his T-shirt was clammy with sweat.

"What was it about?" Aunt Elsa sat on the edge of the bed and patted his hand. "Are your worried about something? Your dad, maybe?"

Chad wouldn't look at her. If he told her about the giant teddy bear, she might laugh. And then she might wonder why he was dreaming about a teddy bear.

He leaned back on his pillow and pulled the sheet up to his chin. "I'm okay," he mumbled. "Honest."

For a while Aunt Elsa just sat there, while he pretended he was going back to sleep. At last, she stood up and tiptoed out of the room, leaving the door open a crack so the hall light shone in.

When she had gone, Chad opened his eyes and stared at the ceiling. He had to stay awake! If he fell asleep and dreamed about the teddy-bear monster again, he knew it would be the end of Weldon and Nichols, famous detectives. He wouldn't be able to make himself go back to Miss Beane's house ever again.

TWELVE

On Guard

It was nearly two-thirty the next afternoon before Aunt Elsa was satisfied with the garage.

"If we've thrown out anything your father wants, that's just too bad," she said crisply. "He should have stayed at home a few evenings and done the job himself. Now where are *you* going?"

Chad's fingers closed over Miss Beane's keys in the pocket of his shorts. "Just around," he mumbled.

"Well, take the dog with you, young man," his aunt ordered. "Looking after that animal is your job, not mine. The poor beast didn't get out of the yard yesterday."

Chad grabbed the leash from its hook and went

outside. Benson lay in the shady spot under the maple tree, his fuzzy bone between his paws. When Chad snapped the leash to his collar, the dog pretended not to notice.

"Come on, boy," Chad kept his voice low, in case Aunt Elsa was listening. "You can sleep when we get there.

"We're not going to crawl through the ditch this time," he told Benson, when they reached Old Oak Road. "We'll keep out of sight on the road and then run fast to the porch. Cap Colby can't be up in his treehouse watching *all* the time."

Secretly, Chad hoped the burglar, whoever he was, wouldn't return. Surely he'd give up pretty soon — unless, of course, he was finding things to steal each time he came. There was no way Weldon and Nichols could tell what, besides the money in the sewing basket, had been taken.

After last night's horrible dream, Chad expected Miss Beane's house to look threatening, but it had a sleepy, contented air in the afternoon sun. *Sort of like Benson,* Chad thought. The dog whimpered with pleasure at the sight of home.

There's no such thing as a live teddy bear, Chad reminded himself as they tiptoed up the front steps of the house. But he held his breath as he unlocked the door, and he looked toward the living room as soon as he and Benson stepped inside.

The teddy bears were where he and Jeannie had left them. The biggest one, not half as tall as the bear in his dream, drowsed against the fireplace bricks.

Chad wondered where he should hide. He'd already decided he wasn't going to tiptoe from room to room this time, peering around corners and peeking into closets. That was just too scary. He'd choose a place — the space behind the big chair in the corner would do — and he would stay there. If the burglar came, he'd try to get a good look at him. If he'd already come and gone this morning — well, a detective couldn't be on duty all the time.

He tiptoed across the living room, pulling Benson behind him.

"Get in there!" He pushed the dog into the corner behind the chair and crawled in after him. It was a tight squeeze. Benson's toes scratched the bare floor as he tried to curl up.

"Lie still!" Chad ordered, forgetting to whisper. Almost at once there was a rush of footsteps upstairs.

Startled, Chad shrank back against the wall and hooked his fingers through Benson's collar. "Now you've done it!" he scolded. "He's here — and he knows we're here, too!"

Benson moaned and scrunched down. Chad waited, not daring to move. He imagined he could hear breathing at the top of the stairs.

"If he comes down, don't you move," he whispered fiercely into Benson's limp ear. "We want to *see* him, and that's all."

Chad peeked around the arm of the chair and watched the stairs for what seemed like forever. His nose itched and his knees ached. He felt as if he were back in his nightmare, hiding and waiting for something terrible to happen.

The floor overhead creaked sharply, and then footsteps moved toward the rear of the house.

Chad struggled to his feet. The back stairs! He'd forgotten about them. He listened in dismay as the footsteps thudded downward into the back hall and beyond, to the basement.

No way! Chad groaned to himself. *I can't follow him down there.* It would be like going into a haunted house, when you knew there was a ghost just waiting to jump out at you.

He was still trying to decide what to do when Benson suddenly climbed over Chad's knees and headed toward the kitchen, barking excitedly. Chad scrambled after him, trying to grab the end of the leash.

At the top of the stairs Benson stopped and stared down into the darkness, his head cocked. Something interesting was down there, he seemed to say, but he wanted Chad to go first.

There was a creaking sound from below, and then a grunt. Chad didn't know what to do. If he stayed where he was, the burglar might get tired of hiding and come charging up the stairs. There would be a fight, and if the intruder was as big as Cap Colby, Chad would be sure to lose. But if he sneaked back to his hiding place behind the chair and let the burglar escape unseen, Jeannie would never let him forget it.

You could have gone down just a few steps, she'd say. You could have had one quick look at him.

Chad edged around Benson and tried again to find a light switch. This time his fingers closed around it. He took one step down, then another, until he had gone far enough to crouch and see the whole basement.

No one was there. The furnace and water heater stood in one corner, with a washer and dryer beside them. On the other wall some boxes were stacked, and there was a low bench against the far wall beneath one of the two windows.

Windows? Chad was surprised. He had been sure there weren't any windows in that inky-black basement. But there they were, and the one above the bench was partly open.

So that was how the burglar had escaped! Chad ran down the rest of the stairs, pulling Benson behind him. At the foot of the steps he paused to check the dim corners once more. Then he ran across the basement to the open window. By standing on the bench and reaching as high as he could, he was able to close the window. He couldn't lock it; the rusted latch had broken.

Chad jumped off the bench and ran back to the stairs with Benson ahead of him this time. They raced up the steps to the kitchen and looked down at the row of bushes that pressed up against the back of the house on each side of the porch. The bushes had given the burglar the cover he needed to slip in and out through the basement window.

Chad was disgusted. If he'd run upstairs as soon as he saw that the basement was empty, he might have seen the intruder make his getaway. If he'd been brave enough to check the basement yesterday, when Jeannie wanted him to, he might have noticed the open window. Now he'd missed his chance. . . .

He started to turn away from the window and then stopped. Something had moved between the lilac bushes at the far end of the yard. He narrowed his eyes and saw a flash of red. *Bright red,* he thought, *like a T-shirt or a scarf — or maybe a baseball cap.*

THIRTEEN

"I Have a Surprise for You. . . ."

"Oh, my!" Aunt Elsa frowned into the telephone. "I don't like to think of you out there all by yourself, dear."

Chad threw himself on the couch and waited for the conversation to end. During the long walk home his excitement had faded, and now he almost wished he hadn't seen that flash of red.

"That was Dora Beane," Aunt Elsa explained when she'd said good-bye. "She's decided to come home Sunday. I don't think she should, and neither does her doctor, but she's going to try it. She'll sleep on the first floor and have a nurse come in for an hour every morning. But what if she fell again?"

Chad sat up straight. Sunday was just two days away!

"What if she feels sick?" Aunt Elsa worried. "What if she can't get around enough to make a meal?"

What if the burglar comes back when she's there alone? Chad shivered.

"She'll be okay, I guess," Chad muttered outside, away from Aunt Elsa's scowl. She thought he didn't care, but he did. He cared a lot! If Miss Beane fell again because someone was prowling around in her house, it would be the fault of Nichols and Weldon, two no-good detectives.

After a week on the case, they still couldn't be sure Cap Colby was the burglar. Jeannie had been right when she said no one would take the word of a parrot. And there must be lots of people in Bristol besides Cap who owned a red baseball cap. The only other clue Chad could add from today's adventure was that the burglar had to be tall and strong. He would have to be at least as big as Cap Colby to hoist himself up and out through that high basement window.

Chad realized that he didn't want Cap to be the burglar. Cap had yelled at them and told them to stay away from his treehouse, but he'd had a right to be angry. And he'd sounded as if he meant it when he said Miss Beane was his friend.

A horn tooted at the end of the block, and the Weldons' truck rattled around the corner. When it screeched to a stop in front of the house, Chad saw Jeannie in the front seat.

"It's not every day I get a chance to give a lift to a pretty young lady," Mr. Weldon chuckled. He gave Chad a quick tap on the head as he ran up the porch steps, two at a time. "I have a surprise for you — something big!" he called over his shoulder. "But first, I have to do a little shopping tonight."

In an instant, Chad forgot about Miss Beane and the burglar. He stared after his dad with a sickly feeling that he knew what the surprise was.

"He's getting engaged," Jeannie whispered breathlessly.

"Did he tell you that?" The question caught in Chad's throat.

"He didn't have to *tell* me. I just know. Didn't you hear him say he was going shopping tonight? He's going to buy Miss Calhoun a diamond ring. I think it's *soooo* romantic!"

Chad felt as if he were going to be sick. "It's not

romantic," he growled. "It's — it's stupid! You're just saying that because he said you were pretty."

He waited for Jeannie to growl back, but instead she sat at the other end of the step and watched him out of the corner of her eye.

"What happened at Miss Beane's house?" she asked, after a while. "Did you see anybody?"

Chad told her about the burglar's escape through a basement window, and his brief glimpse of a red baseball cap. All the time he was talking, he thought about his father and Marcia Calhoun.

"Miss Beane's coming home Sunday," he said. "So we'd better tell somebody about the burglar now."

Jeannie shook her head. "We still have one more day," she said. "I don't have to baby-sit tomorrow, because the twins are having their checkups. We can spend the whole day at Miss Beane's, if we have to."

"We don't have to," Chad said sulkily. "Let the sheriff catch him — that's his job."

Jeannie leaned back on her elbows and closed her eyes. "If we don't catch the burglar," she murmured, "then we're as bad as he is. We've been going into her house without asking if it was all right. Of course, if we could tell the sheriff we actually *saw* the burglar . . ." She sat up and waited.

Chad wondered if anyone had ever been as mixed-up and miserable as he was.

"Okay," he said finally. "One more day's okay, I guess." It was really hard to argue with Jeannie, especially when you were thinking about something else.

FOURTEEN

Some Detective!

"What's going on?" Mr. Weldon stopped cutting his chicken and looked curiously from Chad to Aunt Elsa. "Have the aliens landed? Is the world coming to an end?"

Chad shrugged. Aunt Elsa's face turned pink.

"I'm worried about Dora Beane," she said faintly.

Chad knew that wasn't all she was worried about. His dad had just mentioned *again* the surprise that was coming soon.

"Look on the bright side," Mr. Weldon suggested. "Miss Beane feels so great that she wants to come home. That's *good* news. You can call her every day, once school starts, and Chad can go out there after school and take Benson for walks — maybe do some errands. Between the two of you, she'll be okay."

If she isn't scared to death by the burglar, Chad thought. He shook his head when Aunt Elsa asked if he'd like more roasted potatoes.

"Well, I want some," Mr. Weldon said cheerfully. "A home-cooked meal tastes terrific after a few nights of pizza and hamburgers at the theater."

"I should think so!" Aunt Elsa snapped.

Sometimes it seemed to Chad that he was the father and his dad was the little kid in the family. Most of the time his dad didn't worry about stuff — he just did what he wanted. The rest of the family had to wonder what was going to happen next.

As soon as dinner was over and the table was cleared, Chad went to his room and pulled out his box of baseball cards from under the bed. After a while the front door slammed, and he heard the truck start up.

"Your dad's gone out for a while," Aunt Elsa called. "Important shopping, he says."

Chad didn't reply. For a while, he tried to concentrate on sorting the cards, but he couldn't. Finally, he closed the box and stood up. Benson, sleeping next to the bed, groaned as if to say he didn't want to be disturbed.

"It's okay, boy," Chad whispered. "You don't have to go along this time."

Aunt Elsa was in the living room watching television. "I'm going for a bike ride," Chad told her. "Okay?"

"Kind of late for that, isn't it?" Aunt Elsa raised her eyebrows. "Where are you going?"

"Around."

He expected more questions, but she just nodded. "A half hour's long enough. The days are getting shorter, and I don't like you riding around after dark."

He hurried out to the garage and wheeled his rusty bike down the drive before she could change her mind. The only jewelry store in Bristol was in the mall on the edge of town. It would take seven or eight minutes to get there — ten minutes, maybe, to find out what his dad was doing — eight minutes to bike home again. He could make it if he hurried. Anything would be better than sitting around waiting.

There was still plenty of light as he pedaled across town. Chad waved to people he knew, but his thoughts raced ahead to the mall. When he reached the highway, he stopped to look both ways, then zipped across into the parking lot.

There were several pickup trucks among the rows of cars, but his dad's, older and longer than the others, was easy to spot. Chad locked his bike to the bike stand and hurried into the mall. He couldn't remember where the jewelry store was, so he walked quickly down the brightly lit corridor to his right, all the way to the end. Shoe store, card shop, video store, snack bar — no jewelry store. He turned around and ran back, until a security guard shouted at him to slow down.

The Grand House of Diamonds was the last store at the other end of the corridor. A Going-Out-of-Business-Sale poster hung in the window above a glittering display of rings and necklaces.

Chad stared through the window, his heart thudding as painfully as it had in Miss Beane's house. There were five or six people in the store, but no one he knew.

His dad could have been there earlier, though. Chad glared at one customer and then another, wishing they would go home. At last, when only one woman was left, he slipped into the store. There was a display of diamond rings in a case close to the entrance, and he examined it carefully while the woman paid for her purchases and left.

Then he edged closer to the tall clerk who was drumming his fingers on the counter.

"Well, well, it's the little detective. What brings you here, Sherlock Holmes? Buying a diamond for your favorite girl?"

Chad looked up in dismay. The clerk was Jay Keck, Mrs. Keck's nephew.

"I — I'm looking for my dad," Chad stammered.

"In here?" Jay grinned. In his white shirt and neat tie, and with his curly black hair combed neatly behind his ears, he didn't look like the man who had dragged Chad out from the lilac bushes. Only the mocking little smile was the same.

"I guess he must be someplace else," Chad muttered.

Jay yawned. "You really are some detective!"

"But he could have been here a while ago," Chad persisted, squirming under the clerk's amused gaze. "He's medium-tall and sort of medium-skinny, and he has straight brown hair and glasses."

"That fits at least a half-dozen guys I've talked to in the last hour," Jay snorted. "They all look short to me."

You really are some detective! The jeering words echoed in Chad's ears as he made his way back to the parking lot. His dad's truck was gone. The trip to the mall had been a waste of time.

Except for one thing. Looking at the clerk's tall frame and broad shoulders, Chad had felt a flicker of excitement. Jay Keck was tall enough and strong enough to hoist himself through Miss Beane's basement window. He knew she was in the hospital. And even though he wore nice clothes to work, maybe he needed money.

After all, the Grand House of Diamonds was having a Going-Out-of-Business Sale.

FIFTEEN

Standing Guard

"What do you mean, you won't take the dog?" Aunt Elsa demanded the next morning. "Why not?"

"Because he doesn't want to go," Chad told her, a little desperately. He couldn't tell her that as a detective, Benson was useless. He fell asleep when he was supposed to be on guard. He made noise when he was supposed to be quiet. And he was a first-class coward when there was a burglar in the basement.

Aunt Elsa looked down at the big dog, curled up on the kitchen floor in a patch of sun. "He's supposed to like walks," she said stubbornly. "How do you know he doesn't?"

"Cause he flops down and sleeps every chance he gets. He likes *short* walks. I'll take him around the block when we get home."

"You'll be ready to flop down and sleep yourself by that time," Aunt Elsa retorted, but Chad could tell she was going to give in. "Well, it's your last Saturday before school starts, so I suppose you'd better make the most of it. Wear out your legs, and then maybe you'll be ready to sit at a desk and exercise your brain on Monday."

Chad stuffed a can of soda, an apple, and a ham sandwich into a brown-paper bag. He hadn't actually lied to Aunt Elsa, but he hadn't told her the truth either. He'd said he and Jeannie might go to Riverside Park to see if there were enough kids around to play ball. They might hike out to the dam. They might go to the riding stables to watch the jumpers practice. Those were all things he'd like to do if he didn't have to spend the whole day standing guard at Miss Beane's house.

Jeannie was waiting at the corner, a lunch bag in one hand and a camera in the other.

"I'm going to take a picture of the burglar when he breaks in," she announced. "But first I want to go to Mrs. Keck's house and hear Baby say 'Benson did it' myself. Then we can *both* testify at the burglar's trial." She went on excitedly, "If Cap Colby is watching, he'll see us go there and he'll see us leave — only we won't really leave, of course. We'll hide upstairs in Miss Beane's house, where we can watch her backyard and Cap's yard, too. That's where you should have hidden yesterday."

"We didn't know the burglar was coming in through the basement window until yesterday," Chad snapped. "If you ask me, we're wasting our time. It's our last chance, you know," he added bitterly, but Jeannie just grinned.

"Our last chance to be heroes," she agreed cheerfully. "Wait till you see the Nichols and Weldon Detective Agency on the evening news."

"Weldon and Nichols," Chad corrected her. They didn't speak again until they turned in at Mrs. Keck's driveway.

"Who's that cutting the grass?" Jeannie demanded. "He's really good-looking!"

Jay Keck switched off the mower and ambled across the lawn. "If you're still looking for your father, he's not here," he told Chad. "And if you want to buy a diamond for your girlfriend, I can't help you. Yesterday was my last day in the jewelry business."

Chad scowled at him. "She's not my girlfriend!"

"I'm his partner, sort of." Jeannie giggled. "Is it okay if we visit Miss Beane's parrot?"

Jay bowed and gestured toward the house. "Be my guests. My aunt's gone shopping, but she wouldn't care. Beats me why you want to bother with that boring bird, though."

"Baby's not boring," Chad said. "She's very smart." He stalked up the path to the house, and Jeannie followed him, looking pleased and flustered.

"That guy is so dumb!" Chad stormed when they were safely inside. "I hate him!"

"You said Baby likes soft voices," Jeannie pointed out. "So quit yelling. You'll scare her."

They stood at the dining room door and peered in at the parrot. Baby was perched on top of her cage, looking glum.

"Hi," Jeannie whispered. "Nice parrot."

Baby eyed her for a moment and then turned her back on them.

"You talk to her." Jeannie gave Chad a little push. "Get her to say what she told you before."

"Why?" Chad demanded. "The sheriff won't be-lieve a parrot — you said so yourself. And besides, I don't think Cap Colby's the burglar — I think Jay Keck is. He's tall enough and strong enough and he's had lots of chances to break in and he's out of work —"

"That's crazy!" Jeannie forgot to whisper. "He's not that kind of person. I can tell."

"You *can't* tell! Just because you think he's good-looking . . ." Chad broke off in disgust. He moved slowly around the dining-room table until he was close to the birdcage.

"Hi, Baby," he said softly. "Are you okay?"

Baby looked over her shoulder.

"Say something," Chad coaxed. He reached up and stroked the parrot's head. "I'm your pal, right? Say something."

Baby climbed down the side of the cage and hopped through the open door. "Go home," she muttered mournfully. Then she tucked her head under her wing and pretended to go to sleep.

They waited a couple of minutes, but finally Jeannie had to agree they were wasting their time. "Well, at least she told *you* about Benton," she said, sounding disappointed. "I guess she just doesn't feel like talking today."

"She told us to go home," Chad reminded her as they left the house. "I think she's a smart parrot."

Jeannie made a face. "Don't be such a grouch,"

she scolded. "We've taken care of the first part of the plan, and now we have to do the rest of it. I just hope Cap Colby is watching."

The rest of the plan consisted of walking boldly down Old Oak Road, then doubling back, crouched and darting from one tree to the next. This time Jeannie was even willing to crawl through the drainage ditch until they reached a spot just opposite Miss Beane's front door.

"We have to be absolutely sure Cap doesn't see us going in," she said breathlessly. "We want him to think he can break in any time he wants to."

"We want Jay to think so, too," Chad said, but Jeannie ignored him.

Once inside, they tiptoed upstairs and down the hall to the big back bedroom.

"Hey, look!" Chad exclaimed. Miss Beane's shoes were scattered in front of the open closet door, and one of the dresser drawers was open. "He must have been searching in here yesterday when I scared him off."

"You and Benson," Jeannie reminded him. "I bet he thought there'd be money stuffed into the toe of a shoe."

Quickly they inspected the other bedrooms and

the little storeroom. Nothing else seemed out of place.

"So he's not through looking," Jeannie said, sounding pleased. "He'll be back today."

"Maybe," Chad grumbled. "Or he might not be back for a week."

"Today," Jeannie insisted. "I saw Cap at the library yesterday, and I told him Miss Beane was coming home in a day or so. Now he knows he has to hurry up."

Chad tried not to be impressed with Jeannie's cleverness. "What did he say?"

"He said, 'that's good.'" She smirked. "But he looked really, really upset. He knows this is his last chance to find her money before she comes home."

Chad stationed himself next to the white-curtained window and peeked out. He could see Cap Colby's treehouse, but he couldn't tell if anyone was in it.

"We'll take turns watching," Jeannie said. "And when we see him coming, we'll hide in the bathroom. Then we'll jump out and I'll take his picture while he's poking around in a closet or in the dresser."

She sat on the edge of Miss Beane's bed, careful

not to disturb the worn brown teddy bear that perched in the midst of a pile of ruffled pillows. "What a funny old thing!" she murmured, eyeing the bear thoughtfully. "Maybe he was Miss Beane's own teddy bear when she was a little girl. There are lots of nicer ones downstairs."

Chad stared out the window. He didn't like being in Miss Beane's bedroom without her permission. It felt wrong, even though they were trying to help her.

The long, hot morning passed slowly. Chad wished he had a watch so he'd know how long he'd been standing like a statue next to the window. A drop of sweat rolled down his nose. His T-shirt stuck to his shoulder blades.

"I'll watch for a while now," Jeannie offered at last, when he thought he couldn't stand there another second. "You eat your lunch, and then I'll eat mine."

Chad sank down gratefully and reached for his lunch bag. He wasn't hungry, but the cherry soda would taste good. He popped the can open and took a deep drink.

"Me, too." Jeannie put out a hand without turning from the window. "You can have some of mine later."

Chad wasn't sure what happened next. Maybe his hands were slippery with sweat. Maybe he let go of the can too soon. Whatever the reason, suddenly the can was on the floor, and a stream of soda was pouring across the carpet.

"Oh, no!" Jeannie wailed. "What a mess!" She dropped to her knees and patted the rug uselessly with a crumpled tissue.

Chad ran to the bathroom and grabbed a couple of towels from the rack. He tossed one to Jeannie, and together they rubbed and blotted the wet spot until the towels were cherry-pink.

"We're making a worse mess than the burglar did," Chad groaned.

Jeannie rocked back on her heels. "The carpet's going to be sticky when it dries," she said. "You can get some stain remover from your aunt and clean it up next week sometime — after Miss Beane comes home."

"Why do I have to do it?" Chad demanded. He threw down his wet towel and then snatched it up again. "Why do you get to give all the orders and I do the work? I was handing the can to you, for pete's sake —"

Jeannie scrambled to her feet, her eyes wide.

"Listen!"

Chad froze. For a moment he thought Jeannie was just trying to change the subject, but then he heard it — a distant creaking sound.

"That's the basement window!" he whispered. "He's opening it. We missed him!"

Jeannie grabbed the camera. "Who cares?" she exclaimed. "I told you he'd come — I told you so! Stop looking so scared, silly. Cap Colby's just a kid like we are."

A big kid, Chad thought. *A* very *big kid.* He wished he could crawl under the bed and stay there, but even as he thought about it he was following Jeannie across the hall to the bathroom.

SIXTEEN

*The Burglar —
at Last!*

"**G**et behind the door," Jeannie whispered. "When he starts opening drawers and throwing stuff around, I'll sneak out and take a picture."

"Then what?" Chad demanded. "He'll see the flash."

Jeannie pushed the door, leaving it open just a crack. "Then I run downstairs so he can't grab the camera, and you keep him here till I get help."

Chad stared at her in horror. *"Keep him here!"* he repeated. "How am I supposed to do that?"

"Well, you don't actually have to keep him here, I suppose. But give me time to get away with the camera, okay? The picture will be our main evidence. Sssh!" she hissed, before he could protest. "He's coming up the basement stairs!"

Chad held his breath. This must be how a soldier felt just before a battle. Just before he was going to die.

"If he goes into Miss Beane's bedroom first, he's going to see our lunch bags and those towels," he whispered frantically. "He'll know we're here."

Jeannie rolled her eyes. "Can't help it," she muttered. "Too late now. You should have brought them in here."

They waited. The footsteps halted. Cupboard doors opened and closed. Silverware rattled.

"What's the matter with him!" Jeannie demanded. "Why's he poking around in the kitchen?"

The freezer door *thunked.*

"Come upstairs, you!" Jeannie gritted her teeth. The footsteps moved away from the kitchen, toward the front of the house.

"What a dummy!" Jeannie complained. "He's searching the living room again. I bet he isn't going to come up here at all."

Chad felt a surge of hope, even though he knew what she would say next.

"We'll have to go downstairs."

She opened the bathroom door and peeked out. Chad grabbed her elbow.

"Don't," he begged. "That hall floor creaks a lot."

She shrugged him off and moved out into the hall. At once, the sounds from downstairs stopped. Chad pressed himself against the wall.

After a moment, Jeannie took another cautious step, and this time there was a creak that sounded as loud as a shot in the silence. She jumped back, bumping into Chad. The camera crashed to the floor.

There was a rush of footsteps toward the kitchen. Jeannie snatched up the camera and dashed to the top of the back stairs. Chad peered over her shoulder just in time to see a blue-jeaned leg vanishing down the basement steps.

It is going to be okay, Chad thought. The burglar was leaving. "Come on," he shouted. "You can take a picture of him through the kitchen window."

They hurtled down the stairs and into the kitchen. Drawers and cupboards stood open on all sides, and the contents of the teddy-bear cookie jar had been dumped on the floor. Chad reached the window first and looked down at the row of bushes that lined the back of the house. He could hear a furious scrambling in the basement just below them.

"He'll come out right down there." Chad pointed at a spot in the hedge that lined the back of the house. He was as excited as Jeannie now. "Get ready!"

Jeannie pressed close to the window, but Chad was the one who saw it first — the bright red baseball cap coming around the end of the hedge.

"Over there!" Chad shouted. "Look!"

Jeannie swung the camera to the left, just as Cap Colby's broad face popped into sight. The camera clicked furiously.

"Got him!" Jeannie shouted.

But something was wrong. "What was he doing over there?" Chad demanded. "Why's he sneaking along in front of the bushes like that?"

Jeannie took two more pictures as the red cap bobbed along the hedge and stopped almost below them. Then she lowered her camera.

"What does he think he's doing?" she demanded indignantly. "I want to get a picture of him running away."

At that moment, a second figure burst from between the bushes, directly below the window. Chad caught a glimpse of broad shoulders and a mop of curly black hair. Then Cap leaped forward and dropped a burlap sack over the crawling man's head. The two figures rolled across the lawn, arms and legs thrashing.

"I told you so!" Chad shouted. "That's Jay Keck! Come on! We have to help Cap hold him!"

He dashed to the back door and with trembling fingers managed to turn the key in the deadbolt. He and Jeannie leaped down the porch steps and threw themselves on the burglar's flailing legs.

"Get the rope!" Cap yelped. "In my pockets!" He was straddling the burglar's middle and trying to tug the sack farther down over his shoulders.

Chad scrambled forward and grabbed the lengths of heavy twine that dangled from the pockets of Cap's jeans. Together, he and Cap forced the man's wrists together and twisted the rope around them.

"Now his feet!" Cap gasped. "Hurry up! I can't hold him down much longer!"

"Oh, OUCH!" Jeannie squealed with pain as one of the man's heels caught her squarely in the knee. She rocked backward, close to tears.

Chad threw himself across the burglar's long legs and wound the rope around the man's ankles. With Jeannie's help he pulled the loop tight and knotted it.

Abruptly, the trussed-up burglar lay still. Cap glanced over his shoulder with a dazed expression, as if he hadn't actually realized till then who was helping him. His nose was bleeding, and his face was covered with dirt and blood.

"Call somebody, you guys," he mumbled. "Call the sheriff. He could still get loose!"

For once, Jeannie didn't rush to take charge. "I can't," she gasped. "I feel funny." Her face was a sickly green.

Chad struggled to his feet. His knees shook so badly that he almost fell. He could hardly believe this was happening. Suddenly the detective game had changed into a real battle with a real person. Real people had been hurt.

He staggered toward the steps, but before he could get there, his stomach churned. He leaned over the porch rail and was violently sick.

"Gross!" Jeannie exclaimed behind him, sounding a little more like herself. "Hurry up, Chad. Be sick later."

The telephone was mounted on the side of a cabinet in the kitchen. With a trembling finger Chad dialed 911.

"Hey, Chad, look!" Jeannie called.

He jumped at the sound of Jeannie's voice and almost dropped the phone. Had the burglar gotten loose? He stretched the phone cord as far as it would reach and looked down into the backyard, just as an operator came on the line and began asking questions.

The scene was almost as he'd left it. Cap still straddled the burglar's back. Jeannie was sitting on the burglar's legs, clutching her knee. But the captive had managed to work his way out of the burlap sack and was lying with his head twisted to one side, gasping for breath. As Chad stared, the man's gaze moved upward, and they stared at each other through the window.

It was a face Chad had never seen before.

SEVENTEEN

"You Lied to Me!"

"It was the worst moment of my life!" Aunt Elsa wept. "To see a patrol car pull up in front of this house . . ." She pushed the bowl of spaghetti sauce toward Chad and dabbed at her eyes. "Eat your supper. All I could think was, your father had gone off the road in that broken-down truck, or you'd been drowned in the river." She took a tissue from her apron pocket and blew her nose.

"I'm not hungry," Chad said. "I don't feel so good."

"Well, you don't deserve to feel good." His great-aunt made a lightning switch from tears to anger. "After what you've been up to lately, you should feel as bad as can be."

Chad sank lower in his chair. Aunt Elsa had been crying or scolding ever since the sheriff's deputy had brought him home.

"You lied to me!" she exclaimed for the third or fourth time. "You said you were going to Riverside Park and out to the dam."

There was a strange sound under the table. At first Chad wasn't sure what it was, but then he knew. Benson was getting nervous; he was biting his nails again.

"I said I might go to the park," Chad muttered. "I *might*."

"But you didn't say a word about going to Dora Beane's house, did you? Not a word about stealing her house keys and letting yourself in — what if that wicked man had had a gun or a knife with him?"

"But he didn't," Chad protested. "He was just looking for money."

"And you were going to let yourself and that sweet little Jeannie Nichols get killed to stop him! It's ridiculous, and Dora Beane would say so, too."

Chad wondered how old you had to be before you stopped making big mistakes. He had worried a lot about keeping Miss Beane's burglar a secret, but the possibility of solving the mystery had kept him quiet. Now, with the burglar captured and locked up in jail, he wasn't a hero after all. He and Jeannie and Cap Colby had done something pretty stupid — that was what the sheriff's deputy had said after a second patrol car had arrived and taken the burglar away.

The deputy who remained had boarded up the basement window, and then he'd locked the front and back doors and had herded Chad and Jeannie and Cap into the backseat of his patrol car. They had stopped at the Colby's house first, and the deputy had walked with Cap to the door and had talked for a long time with Mrs. Colby. (It must have been Cap's mother; she stood in the doorway wiping her eyes and scolding, just the way Aunt Elsa was doing now.)

At Jeannie's house, it was her father who answered the door. This time the scolding didn't last very long, because Jeannie had suddenly clutched her knee and started to cry. Chad had never seen her cry before. By the time the patrol car stopped in front of his own house, he was close to tears himself.

Aunt Elsa began clearing the table. "Just wait till your father finds out," she said heavily. "I've a good mind to call that theater and tell him to come home this minute. I can't imagine what he'll say when he hears what you've been up to."

"He'll probably be real late," Chad said hopefully. But before he could carry his dishes to the sink, the familiar chatter and bang of the old truck stopped him.

Aunt Elsa heard it, too. "Now you tell him the whole thing," she warned. "Because if you don't, I will. You tell him how you took the keys and hung around that house and nearly got yourself killed. . . ." She was crying again.

When his father walked into the kitchen, Chad saw that he didn't have to tell. His dad already knew. Either that or he'd lost his job with the parks system!

"I've just spent an hour at the sheriff's office," he said, scowling at Chad. "Along with Jed Nichols and Mrs. Colby. I'd never met her before, but it looks as if we've got the same kind of problem. We all have kids who don't have much common sense!"

Chad slumped back in his chair and stared at his cold spaghetti.

"How'd you find out?" Aunt Elsa wanted to know.

"I got a call from my boss when I was trimming trees at Riverside Park. He said the sheriff wanted to see me about my son. All the way to his office I was thinking, what's happened? I was thinking, maybe Chad's been hurt, maybe he's . . ." He didn't finish the sentence.

Chad slid farther down in his chair. "We — we just wanted to help Miss Beane," he mumbled.

"By keeping quiet when you knew someone was breaking into her house? Some help!"

Aunt Elsa poured two cups of coffee and put them on the table. "You'd better sit down, Bill," she said. "Do they know who the burglar is?"

"A magazine salesman," Mr. Weldon replied. "At least, that's what he claims. He moves from town to town, and the sheriff thinks he's always on the lookout for a likely house to rob. When he got to Miss Beane's that morning, it was just the kind of lonely place he liked. And the front door wasn't even locked. When Miss Beane came downstairs and fell, he got scared off, but he hung around town for a while, asking questions. Someone said Miss Beane probably kept money hidden in the house. So he went back.

"The first time it was easy to pick the lock on the front door, and he found some cash in a sewing basket. The next time the doors were deadbolted, so he prowled around till he saw a warped basement window, and he went in that way." Mr. Weldon rubbed his forehead, as if it ached. "He told the sheriff he wasn't the only one breaking into the house. There were some kids who must have stolen a door key to get in. He didn't find any more money, so he supposed the kids must have gotten to it first."

Chad pushed back his chair. "That's not true!" he shouted. "We never took anything!"

Mr. Weldon nodded. "I don't believe you did," he said. "Neither does the sheriff. But that doesn't mean you were doing the right thing. Poking around in someone else's house, accusing people of burglary — do you know that Benton Colby never thought of playing detective himself until you and Jeannie hinted he might be the thief? He could have been badly hurt with that dumb burlap-bag trick!"

"He was just trying to catch the burglar," Chad said, his voice cracking. "Same as we were."

"Well, there's got to be a better way of getting your picture in the paper," his dad snapped. "You risked an old lady's house and her belongings, and your own lives. There's nothing smart about that!" He paused. "What's that noise in the living room?"

"It's Benson biting his nails," Chad muttered.

"He wants some peace and quiet," Aunt Elsa said. "Poor old fellow."

Mr. Weldon poured himself another cup of coffee. "Why didn't you tell me about the burglar, Chad?" he asked, lowering his voice a little. "We don't keep secrets from each other, do we?"

Chad jumped up. "You do," he retorted. "You keep secrets." Before Aunt Elsa could tell him to watch his tone, he headed for his bedroom. "How could I tell *you*?" he shouted, over his shoulder. "You're never home anymore."

EIGHTEEN

Surprises

The telephone woke Chad the next morning.

"It's for you, Chad," Aunt Elsa called from the kitchen. "Miss Beane wants to talk to you."

Chad pulled the sheet over his head. He'd been scolded by the deputy and by his dad and by Aunt Elsa. He didn't want another scolding from Miss Beane.

"Hurry up," Aunt Elsa said. "It's rude to keep her waiting."

With a sigh, Chad slid out of bed. His legs ached, and there was an ugly bruise on his elbow. He wondered if Jeannie and Cap Colby hurt as much as he did.

"She's coming home today," Aunt Elsa whispered, when he reached the kitchen. "Tell her you'll be glad to take the dog for walks whenever she wants you to."

Chad nodded, but before he could say more than hello, Miss Beane began talking in her sweet, high-pitched voice.

"Chad dear, thank you so much for saving my treasures. The sheriff told me about the burglar and about what you and your friends did. That was very brave of you, dear — foolish, perhaps, but very brave. The teddy bears really are all right, aren't they?"

"Yes, ma'am." Chad was confused. "The burglar wanted money, not teddy bears. He found some money in your sewing basket, so —"

"Oh, that." Miss Beane chuckled. "I always tuck away a few bills to pay the newsboy and the man who mows the lawn. If the thief found that, he found all the cash I had in the house. The truth is, dear — and this is a secret between you and me, Chad — I spend every spare cent on my treasures. Teddy bears can be very expensive, especially the antique ones."

"*Antique* teddy bears?" Chad repeated. He'd never heard of such a thing.

"Oh, my, yes!" Miss Beane exclaimed. "I love my beautiful new bears, of course, but some of the scruffy old ones are special. There's a bear on my bed upstairs that belonged to the child movie actress, Shirley Temple — I paid five hundred dollars for it. And there's one in the living room that was a favorite of President Roosevelt's children. Some people buy stocks and bonds, but I have my treasures right where I can enjoy them every day. Thank you so much for keeping them safe — and for looking after my precious Benson, too."

"Yes, ma'am." Chad wished he could tell Jeannie about the valuable antique bears, but he wouldn't. Not ever. Miss Beane trusted him.

"I can hardly wait to see my Benson and my Baby again," she continued. "I've missed them terribly. And I'm sure they've missed each other, though silly Baby would never admit it. She's such a jealous old thing! Always blaming poor Benson when things don't go the way she wants them to. 'Benson did it,' she'll say, just like a naughty child."

Chad gulped. "Do you mean she says that a lot?"

"Oh, yes, indeed." Miss Beane chuckled. "Every time I drop a spoon or spill some milk, she says, 'Benson did it,' quick as can be. She blames that dog for everything from lost keys to thunderstorms. No doubt she's blaming him now because I've disappeared."

"Yes, ma'am," Chad said. "I think she is." At least he could tell Jeannie about that.

"So if you'll just bring my Benson over to the house this afternoon, dear," Miss Beane went on, "I'll be very grateful. Mrs. Keck is going to fill up my refrigerator with groceries, and that nice nephew of hers will pick me up about three o'clock and take me home."

Chad promised he and Benson would be there.

"Well," Aunt Elsa observed, when he hung up, "you look a little perkier than you did. What was that business about her teddy bears?"

"She was just telling me about them," Chad said, and changed the subject. "Where's Dad?"

"Gone on an errand," Aunt Elsa said. "He'll be back pretty quick."

Chad went to his room to dress and think about Miss Beane's phone call. Nothing was what it had seemed. Baby's "clue" hadn't meant a thing. The treasure in Miss Beane's house wasn't money, it was teddy bears! And even though it had felt good to have her thank him instead of scolding him, he knew that he and Jeannie and Cap weren't really heroes. They were *lucky*!

He was tying his shoelaces when he heard the truck pull into the driveway and stop. A moment later his dad called from the front porch.

"Chad, come on out here. I want to talk to you about something important."

Chad jumped up, then stopped. The surprise! He'd been so busy thinking over what Miss Beane had told him, that for a few minutes he'd forgotten about his dad's secret.

"Mind your manners now," Aunt Elsa said as he passed the kitchen door. She looked at him hard, as if she already knew what the surprise was.

His father sat on the porch steps, waiting. He patted the space next to him, and Chad sat down.

"First thing," his dad held up a finger. "You're grounded for two weeks, except for school and helping Miss Beane with the dog. Got that?"

Chad nodded.

"Second thing. I told you I had a surprise for you — though after what you did yesterday, I about decided to put it off for a while."

Chad looked up hopefully.

"But then I thought it over, and I've decided not

to wait," his dad continued. "You might as well know right now."

"I do know," Chad said through clenched teeth. "I've known right along."

"You know?" His father sounded surprised and disappointed. "How could you know? Who told you?"

As if in answer to his question, Jeannie limped out on her porch across the street and waved. She had a wide bandage around one knee.

"She told me," Chad said. "And we both saw you — at Gormans' Furniture Store. So I know all about it."

Mr. Weldon looked thoughtfully from Chad to Jeannie.

"So that's it," he said softly. "Chad, do you re-member the old story about the boy who had a genie in a bottle? Sometimes I think that kind of genie and your Jeannie are a lot alike. They'll both get you into trouble if you give them a chance." He stood up and pulled Chad to his feet. "Come on. The surprise is in the truck."

Chad followed him around the side of the house with dragging steps. If Marcia Calhoun was waiting in the truck, he didn't want to meet her.

When they reached the truck bed, his dad reached over the side and folded back a tarp.

"Okay," he said. "Look."

Chad stared. A bike lay there — a red and black ten-speed beauty.

"I got it from Marcia Calhoun." Mr. Weldon grinned at Chad's expression. "She gave it to me in exchange for delivering some furniture she bought — at Gormans' — for her new apartment. The bike belonged to her boyfriend in Madison, but he has a motorcycle now so he can come to see her every weekend. All the bicycle needed was new tires, and I ordered those the other night."

"At the mall," Chad said under his breath. "I thought — something else."

"Let's make a deal," his dad said. "It's just possible that someday I might have a secret like the one you were thinking about, but if I do, I'll tell you right away. You won't have to wonder. And if you have a secret that could be dangerous to yourself or to someone else, you'll tell me. Is it a deal?"

"Deal," Chad said. "Thanks!"

Together they lifted the bike out of the truck bed and Chad climbed on. It felt great.

"Would it be okay if I show Jeannie?" he asked. "Just for a minute?"

His dad sighed.

"Jeannie the genie," he groaned. "Some boys never learn." But he laughed when he said it.